perhaps

it starts like this

perhaps in the beginning
there are only colors

red

yellow

then the shapes
come into being
perhaps red says
thank you
and yellow says
hurray
perhaps blue says
nice that I took form

thank you

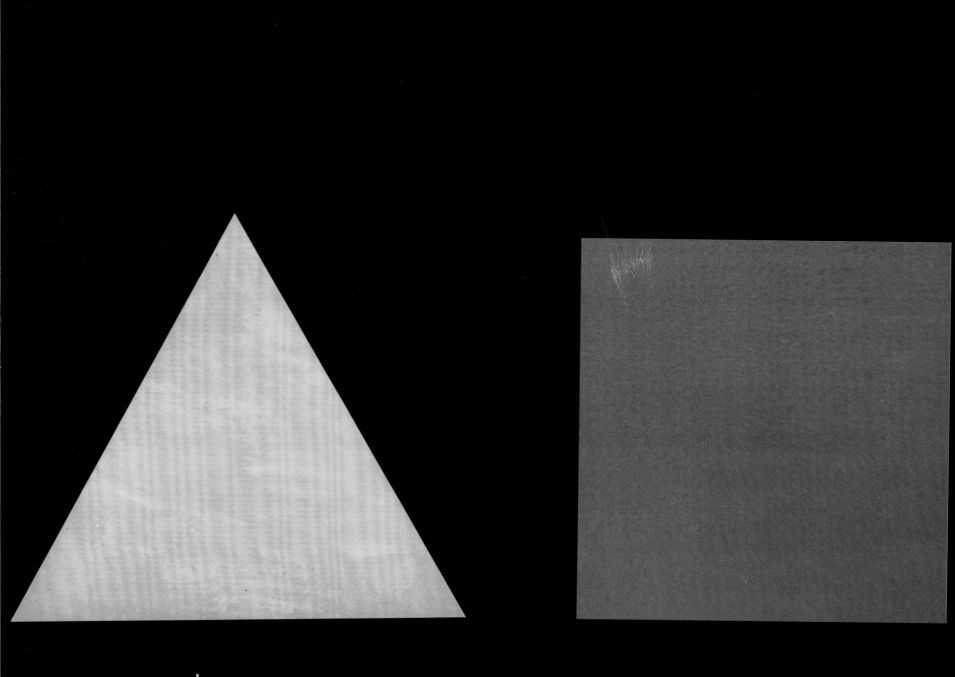

hurray

nice

perhaps
all shapes consist
of smaller shapes
a circle
of small circles
a triangle
of small triangles
a square
(of course) of small squares

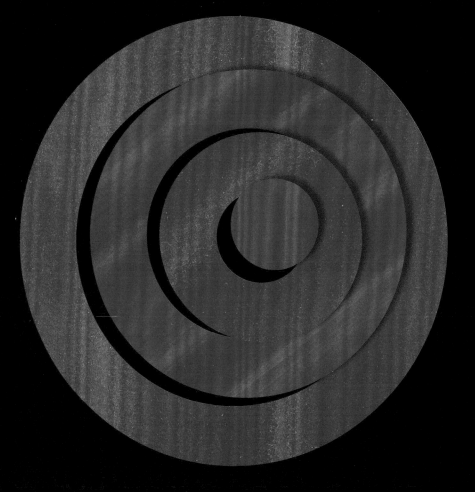

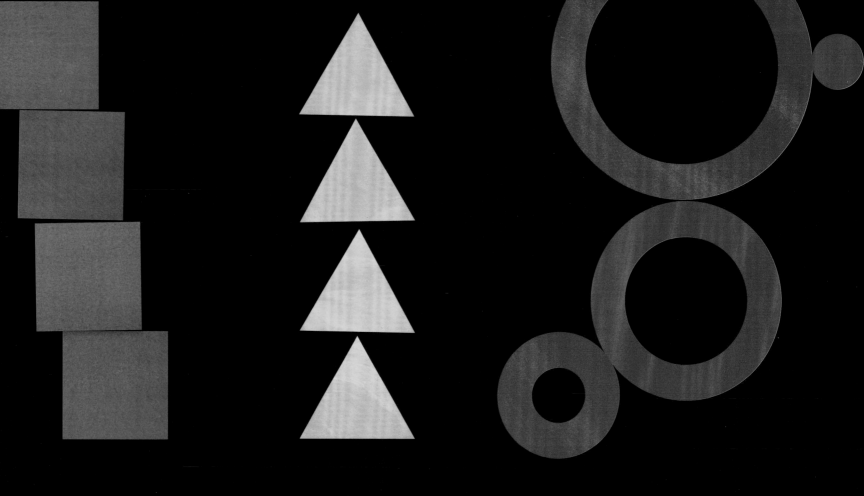

all things   all plants   all animals

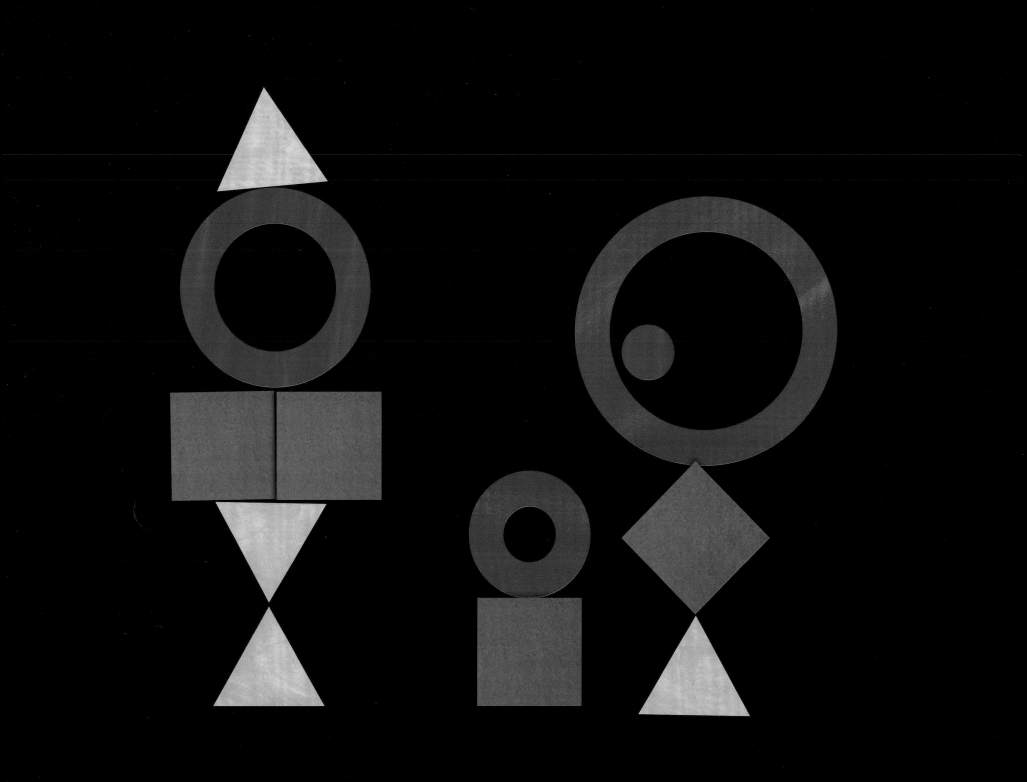

all people

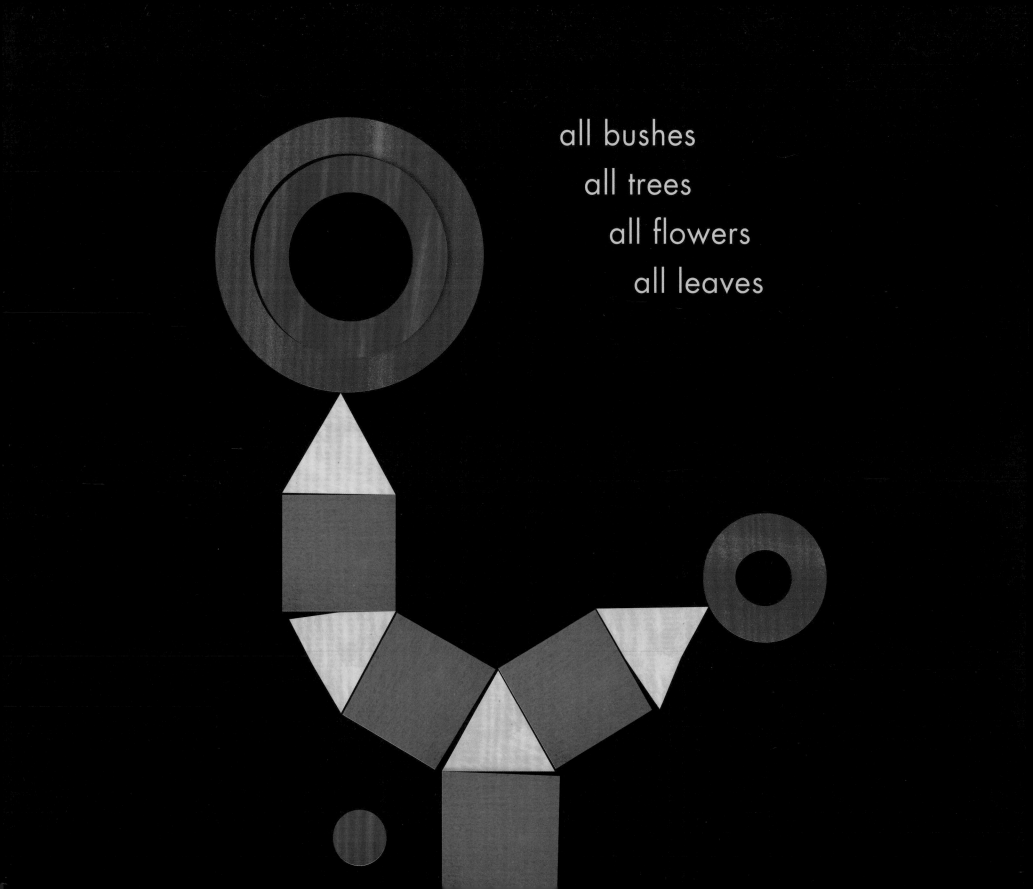

all bushes
all trees
all flowers
all leaves

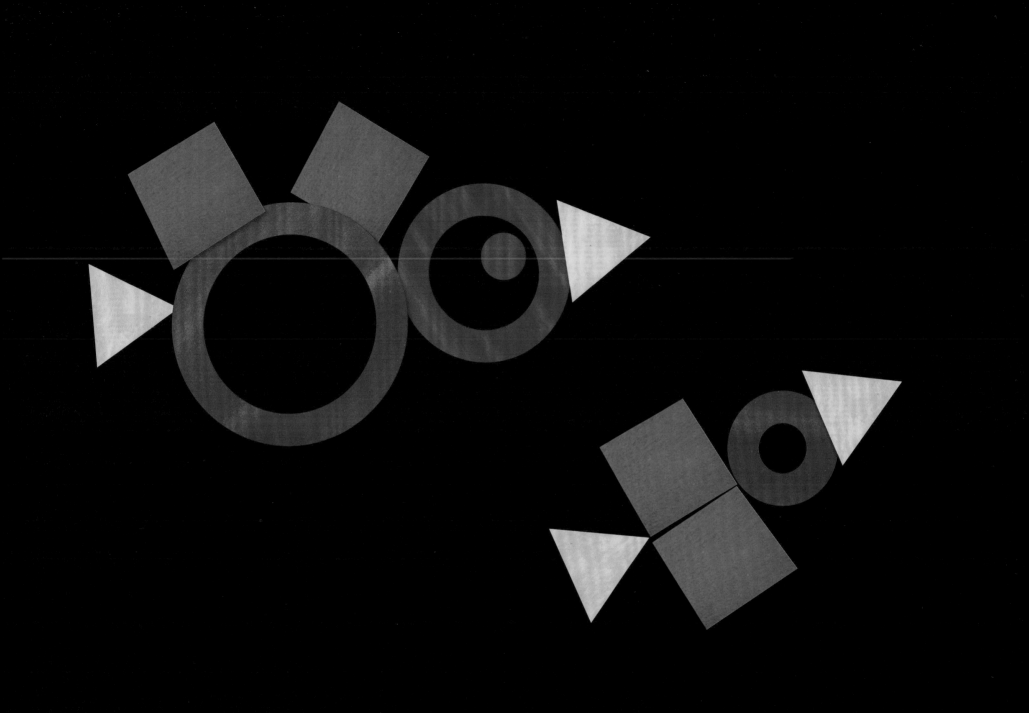

all flying animals

all animals that crawl jump swing and float

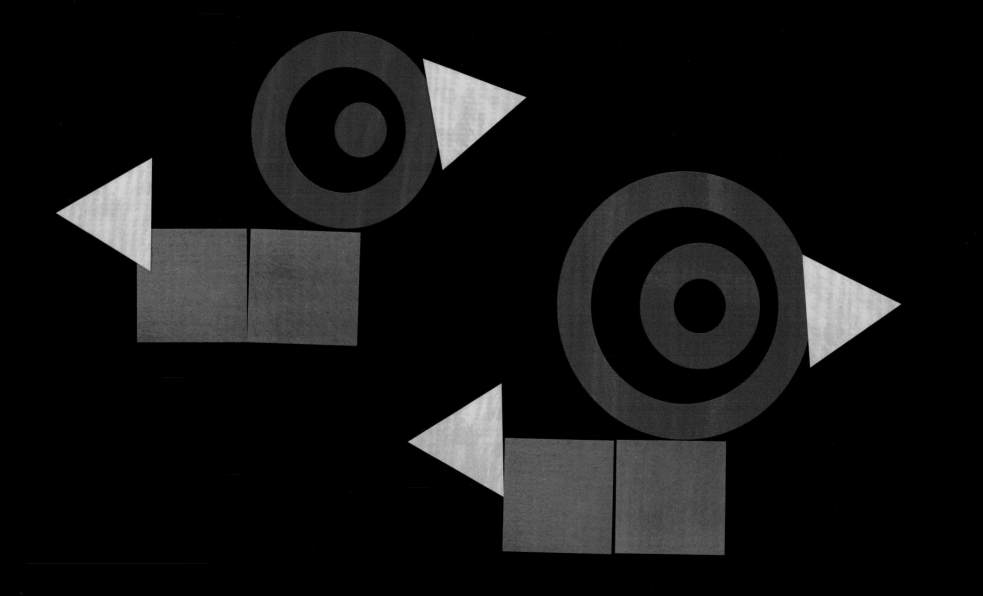

all that roar
bark
growl
and moo

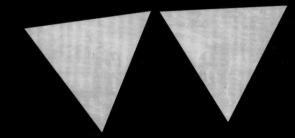
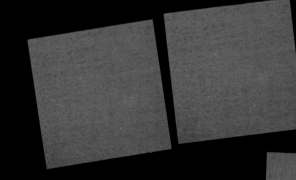
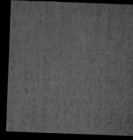

all mommies and daddies

who love each other very much

all children who run ^{jump} shout and sing

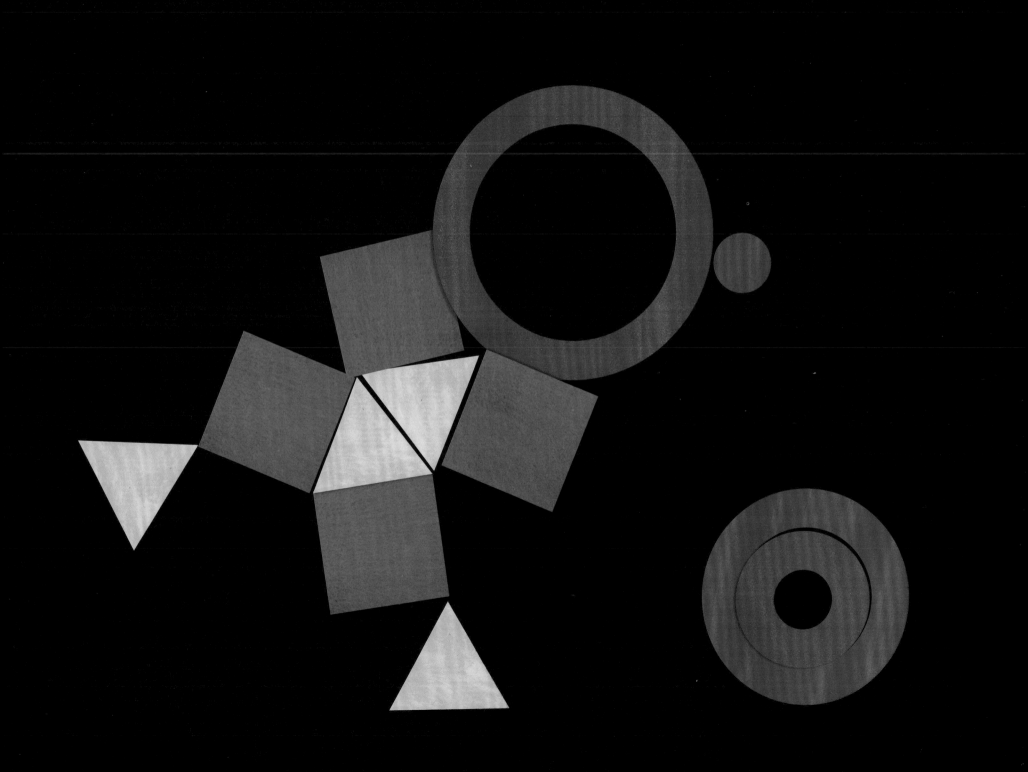

all things
that run on tracks

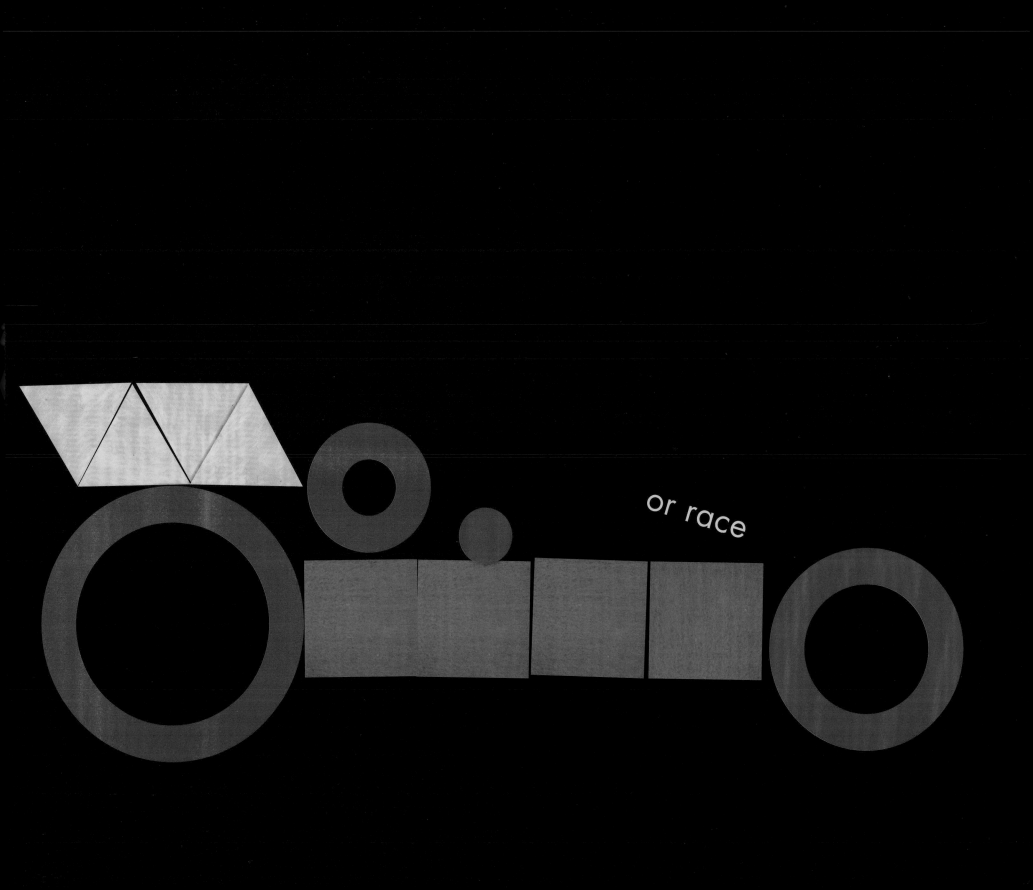

or race

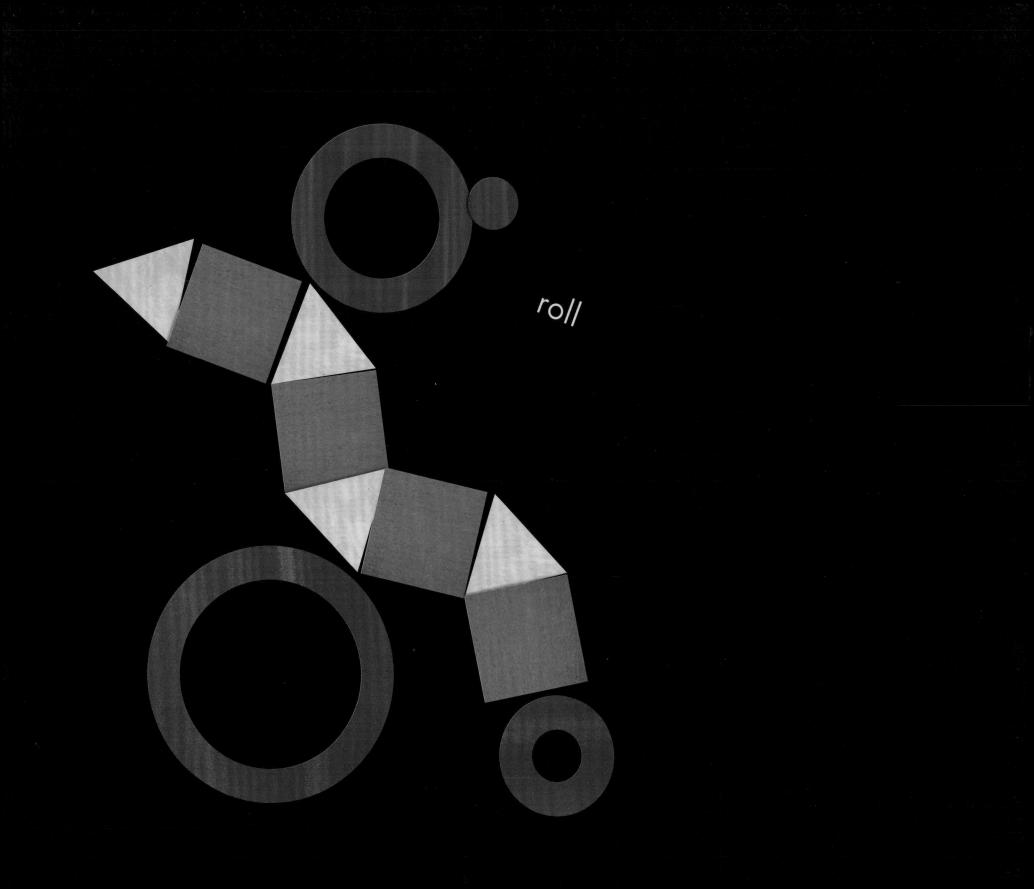

roll

push

and lift

all roofs   all doors   all houses

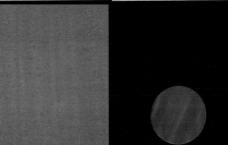
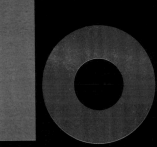

all towers with clocks in all cities

and all strange vehicles
that whizz through deep space

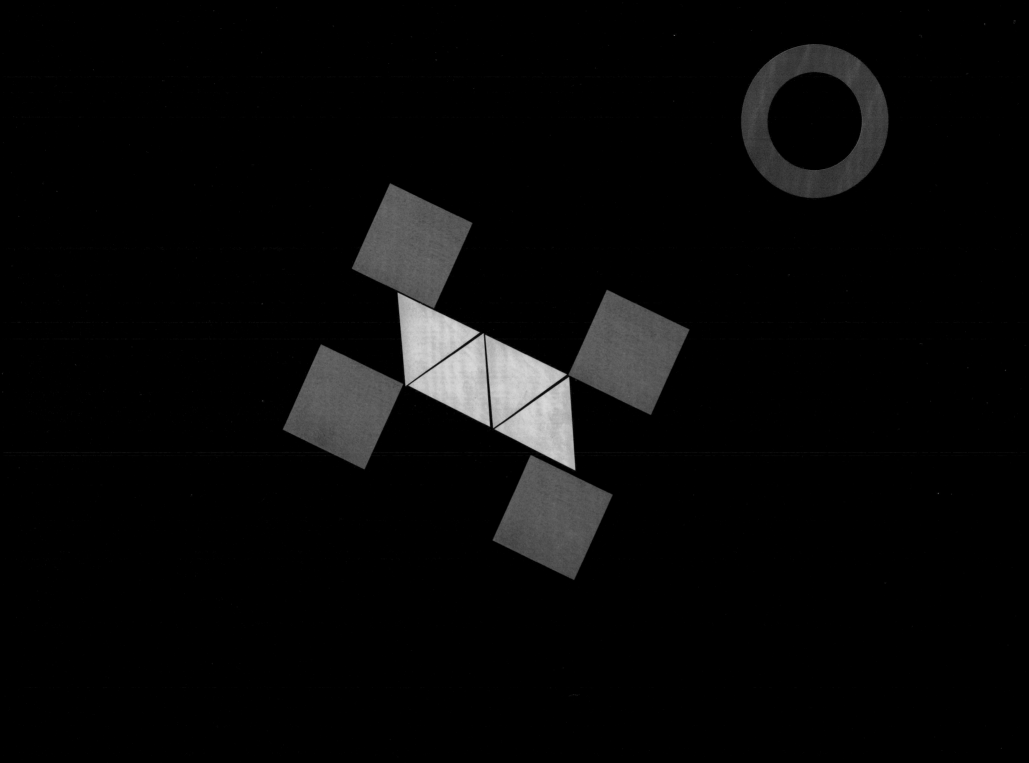

almost as quickly as light

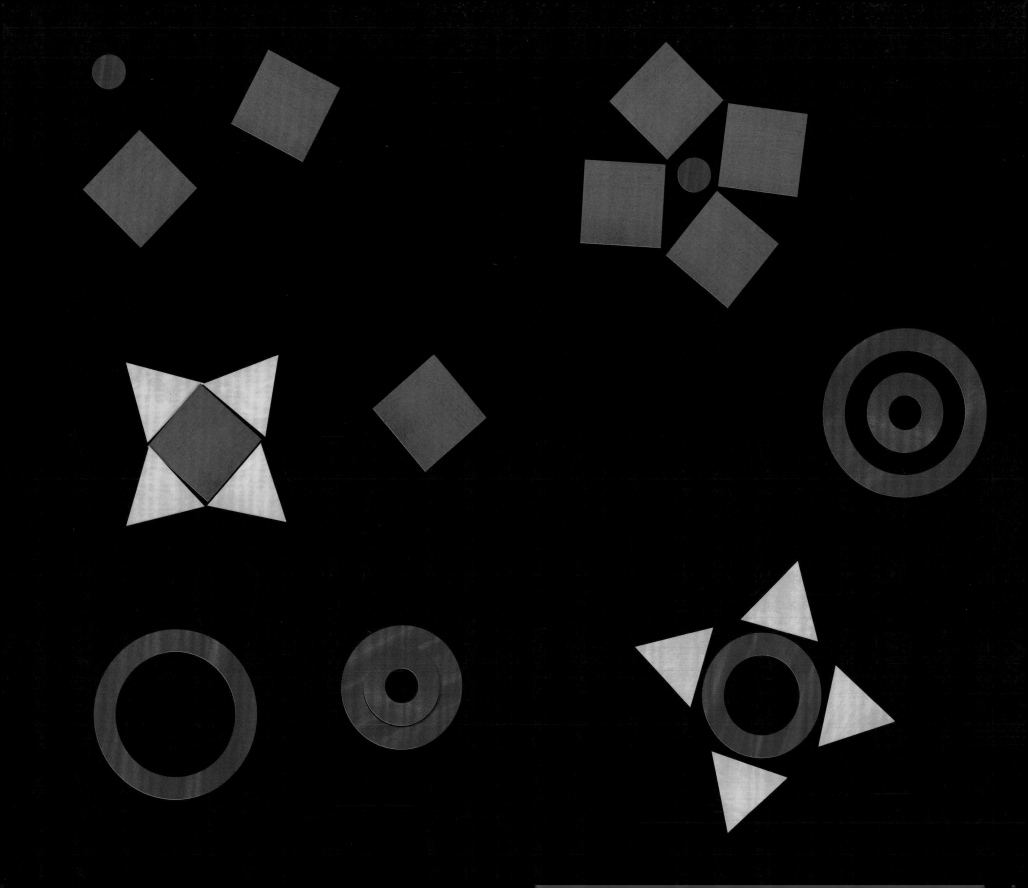

yes perhaps
everything is made
of those small
shapes

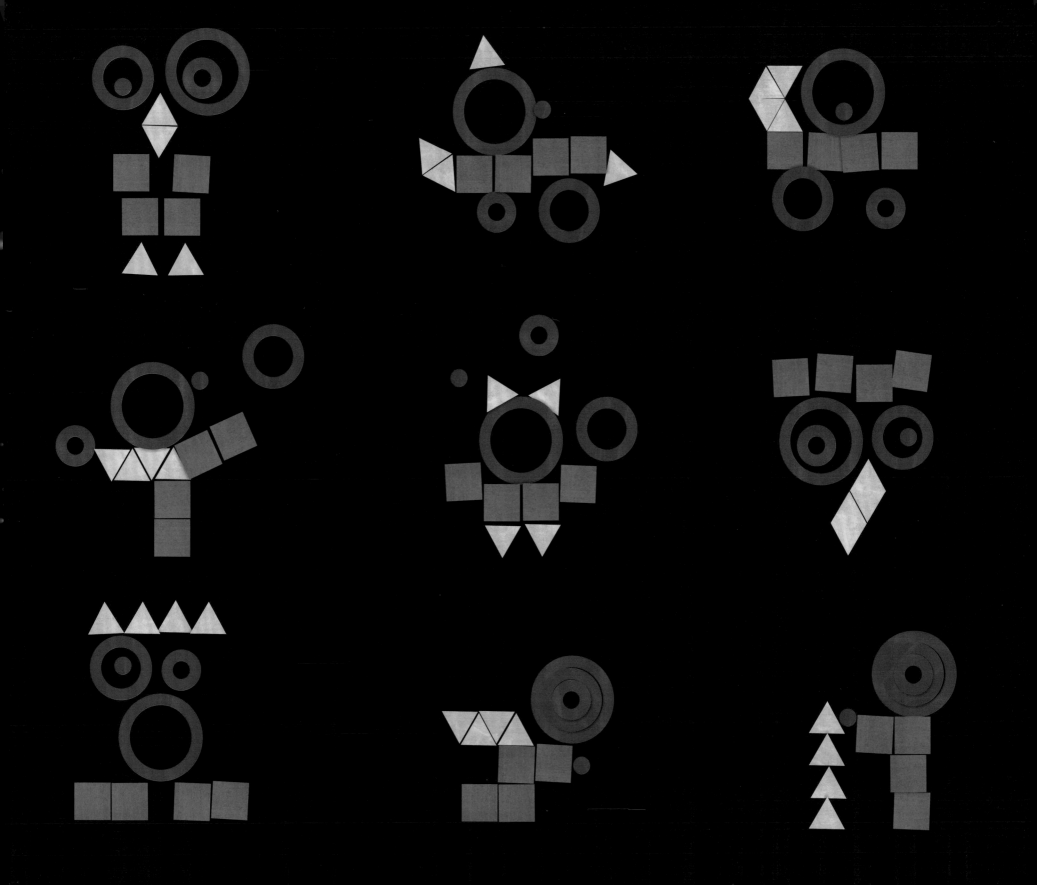

truly everything

all animals all people turn into small shapes again when they die

perhaps those
shapes form
bigger circles
triangles and
squares
and then those turn into

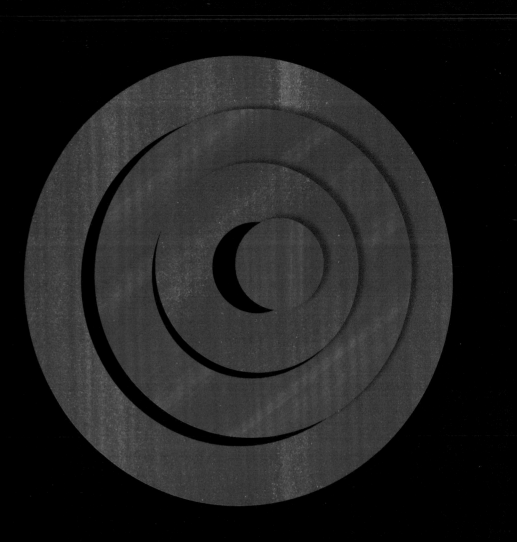

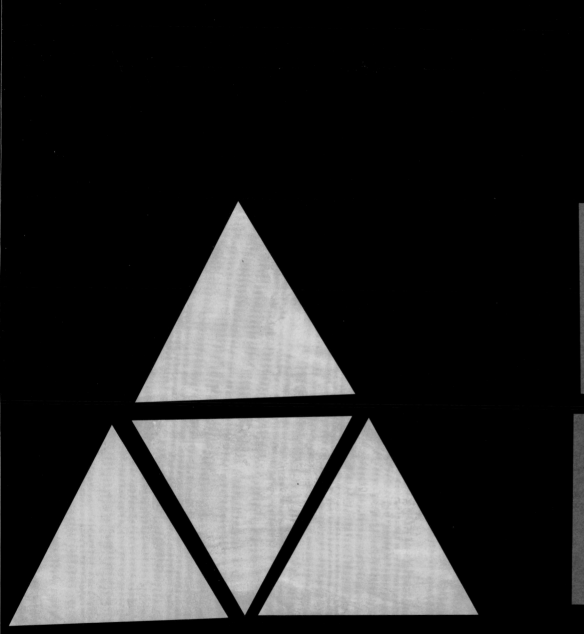

color

over and over

again